First published in Great Britain in 2018 by Pat-a-Cake
This edition published 2019
Copyright © Hodder & Stoughton Limited 2018. All rights reserved
Pat-a-Cake is a registered trade mark of Hodder & Stoughton Limited
ISBN: 978 1 52638 272 6 • 10 9 8 7 6 5 4 3 2 1
Pat-a-Cake, an imprint of Hachette Children's Group,
Part of Hodder & Stoughton Limited
Carmelite House, 50 Victoria Embankment, London EC4Y 0DZ
An Hachette UK Company
www.hachette.co.uk • www.hachettechildrens.co.uk
Printed in China

My Very First Story Time

The Ugly Duckling

Retold by Ronne Randall
Illustrated by Sophie Rohrbach

Ugly Duckling

Mummy Duck

ducklings

wild ducks

reeds

lake

pond

Mother Hen

Granny Goose

swans

children

snowflake

farmhouse

Mummy Duck had sat on her eggs for days and days.
Now they were hatching.

C-r-r-a-c-k! Out came three fluffy, yellow ducklings.
"What lovely babies!" said Mummy Duck.

Then . . . C – R – R – A – C –K, the biggest egg hatched.
Out came a big, grey, fuzzy duckling.

"What a funny-looking baby!" quacked Mummy Duck.

"Time for a swim," quacked Mummy Duck, leading her ducklings to the pond.

"What lovely, fluffy, yellow ducklings you have," clucked Mother Hen.

"What's wrong with that funny-looking one?" honked Granny Goose.

"Nothing at all," quacked Mummy Duck, shaking her tail feathers angrily.

At the pond, Mummy Duck guided her ducklings into the water.

Splish, splish, splish they went as they hopped in.

SPLASH! went the big, grey duckling.

The little, fluffy, yellow ducklings swam very nicely.
But the big, grey duckling was the best swimmer of all!

"Well done!" quacked Mummy Duck, proudly.

The grey duckling grew even bigger than the other ducklings.

"Big feet!" teased his brother.

"Fuzzy feathers!" snapped his sisters.

"Ugly Duckling!" they all squawked at him. "You don't belong with us."

The Ugly Duckling felt so sad and alone, he decided to run away.

The Ugly Duckling went to the lake. Some wild ducks were swimming near the shore, quacking happily and shaking their feathers.

"Can I stay here with you?" he asked, hopefully.

"No!" replied the wild ducks, nastily. "You are not one of us.
Go away!"

As the Ugly Duckling swam away sadly, he looked up.
A flock of white birds with long, graceful necks was flying
across the sky. They were the most beautiful birds he had
ever seen.

"I wish I looked like them," thought the Ugly Duckling.
"Then everyone would like me!"

Gradually, the lonely days became shorter and the freezing, frightening nights grew longer. Winter had arrived, and when the lake froze, the Ugly Duckling couldn't find any food. Alone, he huddled on the cold ground and fluffed his feathers to try to keep warm.

When it snowed, the Ugly Duckling, shivering and shaking with cold, waddled along until he came to a farmhouse. It was warm and cosy, but the children who lived there were rough and noisy. The Ugly Duckling was frightened and ran away, back to the icy lake. He was alone again.

The winter was long and lonely, but at last spring came and the warm sun melted the frozen lake. The Ugly Duckling slid into the water. Looking down, he saw his reflection.

"Who is that handsome creature?" he wondered.

All at once, the beautiful birds he had seen in the sky flew down beside him.

"What a handsome swan you are," they said.

The Ugly Duckling wasn't ugly after all. He was a SWAN!

Spreading his great, white wings, he launched into the air with his new family. He knew he would never be lonely again.

Help the Ugly Duckling find his way from the farmhouse to the lake.

Can you spot five differences between these two pictures?